THE IMMORTAL ROOSTER AND OTHER STORIES

Diane de Anda

With Line Drawings by Roberta Collier-Morales

PIÑATA BOOKS
ARTE PÚBLICO PRESS
HOUSTON, TEXAS
1999

This volume is made possible through grants from the National Endowment for the Arts (a federal agency), Andrew W. Mellon Foundation, and the City of Houston through The Cultural Arts Council of Houston, Harris County.

Piñata Books are full of surprises!

Piñata Books
An Imprint of Arte Público Press
University of Houston
Houston, Texas 77204-2174

Cover illustration by Roberta Collier-Morales
Cover design by Ken Bullock
Interior illustrations by Roberta Collier-Morales

de Anda, Diane.
The immortal rooster and other stories / Diane de Anda.
p. cm.
Summary: A collection of stories which reflect the joys and disappointments of a variety of young Mexican Americans.
ISBN 1-55885-278-6 (pbk. : alk. paper)
1. Mexican Americans — Juvenile Fiction. 2. Children's stories, American. [1. Mexican Americans — Fiction. 2. Short stories.] I. Title.
PZ7.D3474Im 1999
[Fic]--dc21 99-10498
CIP

∞ The paper used in this publication meets the requirements of the American National Standard for Information Sciences—Permanence of Paper for Printed Library Materials, ANSI Z39.48-1984.

Printed in the United States of America

9 0 1 2 3 4 5 6 7 8 0 9 8 7 6 5 4 3 2 1

Contents

To my parents,
Salvador and Carmen de Anda,
in appreciation for their
loving presence and support,
for their strength in life and courage in death.

The Immortal Rooster

Based on a True Story

Grama Nacha pulled into the driveway quickly. She wanted to take the rooster out of the trunk of her car before it could leave a mess that would make her sorry she ever bought it. She called to her two grandsons, who were playing kickball on the lawn. After all, she thought, taking the rooster out of the trunk was going to be tricky.

Grama gave the boys instructions in a serious tone: "Okay, boys, when I open the trunk, I want you to make sure the rooster doesn't jump out until I can get a good hold on him."

The boys could not believe what they were hearing. This was the west side of Los Angeles, after all, not some country barnyard. How could their grandmother possibly have a rooster in her trunk?

Grama noticed the puzzled look on their faces. "I've just come from the pound. They had these two roosters and said they'd sell them to me for fifty cents apiece. So, I bought them—one for all of you, and one for me. But they only had one box, so I had to put the other one in the trunk."

That made perfect sense to the boys, so they took their places, arms forward, palms up, in front of the trunk.

"Now when I open the trunk, wave your hands and make noises to scare him back in," Grama directed.

The trunk door made a popping sound as it lurched upward. The lanky orange and black bird scrambled across the trunk at the sudden noise and rush of sunlight. Immediately, the boys lunged forward. They frantically waved their arms and let out a chorus of yelps, growls, and screeches that frightened the bird away from the opening.

Grama Nacha remembered how as a young girl in Mexico she had been sent out into the yard to pick and pluck that night's supper. In an instant, she reached into the trunk, snatched the rooster by the feet with one hand, and grabbed its neck with the other. She called to the boys to close the trunk. Together they leapt up and sent the lid crashing down.

By now the neighbor children had heard the commotion, and three of them rushed over to see the struggling rooster. Grama Nacha walked up to the front door in Pied Piper fashion, the small band following her and her captive.

Grama nodded her head toward the door. The two boys scrambled around her, threw open the door, and dashed in ahead calling to their parents, "Mom, Dad, come here quick and look what Grama's got!"

Carmen and Sal looked up from the dining room table to see Grama Nacha walk into the front room carrying the wiggling and complaining rooster.

"Oh my God, Mama," gasped Carmen as both she and her husband leapt to their feet. "Drop it; drop it before it pecks you."

"*Ay, m'ija,*" she replied. "I used to do this when I was just seven years old."

Sal took quick steps to the sliding glass door and flung it open. "Here, Nacha, let him go out here," he called to her.

Grama Nacha took a few quick paces across the front room and out onto the patio. Her two granddaughters, who had been peering through the glass door at all the activity, quickly moved out of her way. She bent forward and eased the bird's feet onto the cement floor. Happy to be free, the rooster began to strut around his new surroundings. He jerked his head back and forth as he surveyed the patio, the yard, and the growing crowd of onlookers.

The young boys laughed and dared each other to grab the rooster's tail feathers. They followed him at a safe distance, making jerky neck movements. The rooster kept moving, edging away from anyone who approached.

The adults watched for a while. But soon they grew tired of all the movement and noise and scooted the boys off of the patio and into the front yard.

Carmen handed the girls pieces of dried bread. "Here. Roosters don't like to be chased," she explained. "Just let him walk around and throw him pieces of bread."

The two girls tossed out small pieces to the bird. First they threw them across the patio to him. But little by little, they brought the feeding area closer and closer to them. In a few minutes, he was happily pecking at the tiny pieces they dropped in a semi-circle in front of them.

They studied his handsome, shiny, dark feathers. The feathers lay sleek against his body and ended in a beautiful curly black and orange fan. The girls watched the red comb dance above his eyes as he ate. Meanwhile, his yellow eyes stole glances at them to make sure they remained still and farther than an arm's length away.

Six-year-old Marta decided to greet their new guest.

"*Ki-kiri-kí, Ki-kiri-kí,*" she crowed in her best rooster-like voice.

"That's it—that's the perfect name," interrupted her ten-year-old sister Celia. "We'll call him Kiki."

As the girls discussed their new pet, the adults at the dining room table were also discussing his future. They had already decided on a name for him: Sunday dinner.

"Mama, what ever possessed you to buy us a rooster?" Carmen began.

"Where can you buy Sunday dinner for the whole family for only fifty cents?" her mother quickly replied.

Sal just grinned, knowing he could never predict what his mother-in-law would do next. Suddenly, they were interrupted by the rooster's loud crowing. A neighbor's cat had leapt onto the backyard fence. The terrified rooster had begun running in wild, zigzag lines across the patio and yard, crowing his fear for all the neighborhood to hear.

"The neighbors, the neighbors! Quick, shut him up before someone calls the police," Carmen pleaded with her husband.

Sal dashed out into the patio and began to chase after the bird, which was now even more panicked. The patio was filled with the sounds of Sal and the bird scuffling back and forth across the yard, broken crows from the rooster, and high-pitched screams from the girls. Finally, Sal cornered the rooster against the fence and reached forward to grab him. Just as he did, the rooster flapped his wings and jabbed Sal's hand with his beak. Sal pulled back instantly as he felt the sharp peck on his knuckle. He hesitated a moment as he noted the droplets of blood forming.

"That's it! Sunday dinner's going to come a little early," he announced to the rooster as he leapt forward and wrapped his fist around the bird's neck. The bird thrashed a short time at the pressure of the thick, strong fingers, but soon fainted in his grasp. His head drooped across Sal's hand.

The girls froze and gasped in disbelief. After all, this was the father who carried puppies zipped up in his jacket against his body to keep them warm; who had once stopped his truck on the freeway shoulder to rescue a wounded seagull; who gently cleaned and bandaged their cuts and scrapes. They had not understood how clear the difference was for him: There were pets and people, and then there was dinner.

Their mother and grandmother approached the girls. Carmen put her hands on their shoulders, "I'm sorry you had to see this. Maybe you should go up to your rooms for a while," she suggested.

Grama Nacha took a different tack.

"When I was your age, my mother would send me into the yard with an axe to kill and pluck the chickens. Besides, the same thing happens to the chicken you buy at the grocery store," she reminded the girls.

The girls protested, "It's a very different thing to eat someone you know personally!"

The discussion ended with the *thud* of the rooster as their father dropped it onto the ground and walked back into the house. The two women followed, leaving the girls staring at the limp body at the edge of the patio. "Kiki," they whispered as tears filled their eyes. Cautiously they approached. As they got within three feet of the rooster, he began to move and rustle about. Amazed at the sight, the girls stood in hushed silence. In a few seconds, the rooster opened his eyes and pulled himself to his feet.

The girls cheered spontaneously as the rooster bounded away from them. The adults heard the girls and looked out just in time to see the rooster hurry off the patio and into the yard. Disbelief on their faces, they rushed to the patio together, Sal in the lead.

"I don't believe it! I swear he stopped breathing right in my hand." Sal looked down at his strong, leathery hands. These were hands that lifted two-hundred-pound crates of produce with ease. These were hands with a grip that could take most men to their knees. Certainly no bird could challenge the power of his grip.

This time the rooster didn't run away so fast and was easily snatched by the neck. Sal pulled his fingers together in a vise-tight grip, shaking the bird until bone-cracking noises could be heard. Meanwhile, their mother kept the girls from watching their father and the bird by holding their faces against her.

With the pride of victory, Sal threw the bird down onto the patio cement with such force that it bounced in front of him. Satisfied that his job was now completely done, he walked across the patio toward his family. He reached them just in time to hear his wife gasp, "Oh my God, he's still alive!"

Sal turned on his heel just as the rooster pulled himself to a standing position. Sal's emotions passed quickly from disbelief to anger at the insult he had received from this cunning bird. Now it was truly a contest, with much at stake for each.

Still somewhat dazed, the rooster was easy to catch. This time Sal was going to make sure the job was done right. He spun the rooster by the locked grip on his neck. He twisted, shook, and squeezed the bird. Finally, he curled his fingers into his hand and applied firm, steady pressure for two full minutes until the bird lay limp and lifeless in his grasp. He then casually dropped it onto the patio and went inside the house without a word.

"It's all over," their mother whispered to the girls, who had been quietly weeping against her. Their mother and grandmother tried to urge them into the house, but the girls insisted on staying outside with the bird for just a few more minutes.

He was beautiful and still with his shiny black feathers reflecting the sun. For a moment they even considered each keeping a tailfeather as a momento, but the idea of actually pulling a feather off the dead creature seemed too ghoulish and disrespectful. They edged closer and studied his lip-red comb, the pale shiny yellow beak. And then, to their astonishment, the rooster's body began to twitch. They had heard about chickens running around with their heads cut off, so they instantly backed away. In a few minutes, the quivering stopped and the rooster lifted himself back onto his feet.

"Yay, Kiki! Yay, Kiki! Yay, Kiki!" they began to crow about the patio. The adults looked into the patio through the sliding-glass door in response to the commotion and saw the two-legged phantom slip off the patio and into the back yard.

Sal felt the heat rise to his face. His muscles twitched as the surge of anger jolted him to his feet and quickly out onto the patio. This time the girls stood side by side, their arms out as barriers between their father and the rooster.

"Three times a charm! Three times a charm! He wasn't supposed to die," they cried. "He's no ordinary rooster; he came back to life three times."

Sal looked over at the immortal rooster strutting with a slightly bent neck across the backyard, and all the anger and drive he had felt vanished. This rooster could never be a pet, but certainly such a determined creature could also never be just dinner. And so the girls and their father came to an agreement. Sal packed the rooster in an empty celery crate and drove him out to a local produce farm. Though not truly immortal, the rooster lived a long life roaming through fields of cauliflower and celery and green beans. And as each day began, he raised his wiley, bent neck to crow his challenge into the morning sun.

DANCING MIRANDA

Miranda didn't dance to the music. Miranda *became* the music, her heartbeat one with the rhythm that carried her across the floor. She turned in beautiful, perfect circles, swiveling with ease on the balls of her feet. She bobbled across the floor on tiptoe. She seemed to hover above the ground as she sailed across the floor in long flying leaps.

She had danced in the park, gliding across the grass and blacktop. She had danced on her patio, in almost every room in her house, and in the houses of friends and relatives. She had even danced on the shiny wooden floor at her aunt and uncle's wedding reception. But she had never danced on a stage before. Now, in a few days, she would dance on a big stage at the Music Center downtown. She would dance in front of the mayor and hundreds of people to celebrate Children's Day.

Miranda had practiced her part every day for two months by herself in the long hall down the middle of her house. She had practiced with her group after school to the *tap, tap, tap* of the dance teacher's cane on the wooden floor.

Tap, tap, tap. The ten girls moved together, a

single wave moving in perfect rhythm back and forth across the floor. As the music became louder and faster, Miranda twirled in tight little circles away from the rest of the dancers to the front of the group. Miranda felt the music surround her. The music became a gentle whirlwind carrying her in perfect flowing arcs around the other dancers. She leapt across the floor in powerful scissor kicks that ended in a slow, delicate glide back to her place in the group. The music swept the group forward in little prancing steps. They lifted and curved their arms high above their heads and swayed side to side. Together they made one more dip to the side, then spread their arms and glided into their last spinning turn, which ended in a bow.

Their teacher, Mrs. Sommers, hooked her cane on her arm and began to applaud, "Perfect, just perfect, girls," she called out as she continued to clap her hands. "Now, girls," she said, as she took her cane off her arm and leaned forward on it toward the group, "I want you to be prepared for what you'll see when the curtain goes up."

Mrs. Sommers motioned the group to come closer so she could read their feelings by looking into their eyes as she spoke. "When the curtain goes up, suddenly there will be bright lights above you and spotlights from across the theatre. The rest of the theatre will be very dark, so that you and the stage will shine as bright and beautiful as stars on a dark night."

The girls' eyes opened wider as she described them on the stage.

"Now, if you look beyond the stage you will see people smiling at you from the rows in the audience."

"How many people?" Inez asked in a soft and hesitating voice.

"Well, it is a very big theatre, and it's a special celebration, so there are going to be many, many people there," replied Mrs. Sommers, watching the girls' faces as she spoke.

The girls' eyes began to shift as they shared glances with each other.

"But I want to teach you all a special trick so it won't matter to you whether there's one or one thousand people out there."

The girls edged in closer and Mrs. Sommers bent at the waist towards them as she spoke in slow, exaggerated tones. "The trick is to pretend that the stage really *is* a star, and that you're dancing together on this beautiful shining star, floating somewhere by yourselves in the heavens. All you have to do is keep thinking about the music and moving to it together. Close your eyes and picture it now."

The girls all closed their eyes and rode the glimmering star in dancing daydreams.

In a few minutes, Mrs. Sommers brought them back to earth. "Okay, girls, that's all for today. Remember, rehearsal tomorrow at ten o'clock sharp."

Inez and Miranda walked over to a bench in a corner of the studio and changed into their street shoes.

"I hope it works," said Inez, shaking her head.

"What works?" replied Miranda as she yanked the laces on her pale blue leather tennis shoes.

"You know, pretending that we're in space dancing on a star so we don't have to think about the hundreds of eyes staring up at us." Inez took a big swallow.

"I guess it might," shrugged Miranda. But Miranda knew that she didn't need a trick, that the music always carried her shooting like a star across the sky.

The Saturday morning sun pushed its way through the slats on the mini blinds and threw stripes of light across Miranda's face. She sat up and smiled as she remembered how it felt in her dream to be leaping from star to star across the sky. She jumped out of bed and took hopscotch leaps across the linoleum squares, pretending she was still sailing across the sky. By the time she got to the bathroom sink she felt a little flushed and giddy.

Miranda usually slept late on Saturday mornings, but today she was dressed in her blue leotard and shiny satin dancing shoes by eight o'clock in the morning. She was ready to dance her way through the day. She danced the cereal bowls into place around the kitchen table. She tip-toed up to the large cat sitting by the stove. He raised his broad orange striped face towards her and followed her with his wide yellow eyes as she twirled and bowed low enough to sprinkle the dry catfood into his bowl.

It was hard for Miranda to sit still in the car on the way to rehearsal, so she tapped her dance slippers together and did little toe dances on the car floor as they drove. Finally they arrived at the Music Center, and her mother parked the car. Miranda held onto her mother's hand as they walked up the ramp to enter the building, but she was so excited that she kept moving ahead of her mother, tugging her along.

Her mother laughed, "Go on ahead, Miranda. I'll catch up with you inside."

Miranda gave her mother a quick smile, let go of her hand, and bounded forward in great skipping leaps up the ramp, across the red and gold carpet in the lobby, down the long side aisle, and up the steps onto the stage. Miranda felt herself slide across the hard shiny floor. In a few minutes Inez and the other girls arrived and joined her on the stage, laughing as they all practiced little leaps and pirouettes.

As Miranda moved toward the edge of the side curtains, she could hear her mother and her dance teacher talking.

"It's an inborn talent, a gift, Mrs. Montero. Were you such a dancer also as a girl?" Mrs. Sommers smiled warmly at Miranda's mother.

"I did a lot of dancing in my daydreams, but I couldn't move like my Miranda." Mrs. Sommers noticed Mrs. Montero's eyes cloud slightly as she continued. "I had polio as a young girl and wore braces on my legs until I was way into my teens."

"Oh, I'm sorry. I didn't mean to pry," Mrs. Sommers began.

At that point Mrs. Montero noticed Miranda, who had been standing just inside the curtain. Unaware that she had heard their conversation, Mrs. Montero excused herself and walked over to Miranda.

"Here, *m'ija*," she said, as she pushed her daughter's hair away from her face and clipped it in place with the two barrettes she had in her hand. "This will let you see where you are going when you twirl across the floor. I'll be sitting in the front row ready to clap real loud. You'd better get back with your group now." She winked at Miranda, and Miranda managed to turn the corners of her mouth up slightly.

Miranda watched her mother as she walked back and continued talking with the teacher. She looked at her mother's shoes—simple, plain flats, not like the square or slender heels the other mothers wore. But she had never thought about it before. Her mom was simply her mom, just the way she was. She had never thought of her as different. Certainly she had never thought of her mother as a young girl. But now she could picture her mother as a child sitting alone as the other children sailed by her just as Miranda did, gliding so easily and lightly across the ground. She could see her mother's feet hidden in coarse, brown, laced shoes that looked almost nailed to the ground. She remembered now a few pictures of her mother as a little girl smiling in a group of girl cousins at a birthday party. She remembered the silver braces on the heavy brown shoes that looked so odd beneath the full skirt of her pink ruffled party dress. Miranda bent one leg up at the knee and gracefully extended it out. She imagined the weight of thick shoes and braces, and her leg dropped stiff and heavy as a rock to the ground.

"Everyone take your places. Quickly, quickly," Mrs. Sommers called to the group.

Miranda hesitated a moment as she watched her mother hold on to the guardrail to steady her balance on the steps down from the stage.

"Come on, Miranda, come on and get in line. We're on first," said her friend Inez tugging on her arm.

"Okay, okay, I'm coming," she called as she trailed slowly behind Inez, who skipped with excitement to her place in the line.

In the dance studio they took up the whole floor. Now on the big stage Miranda felt dwarfed by the huge curtains and the high ceilings with the bright lights. She looked out over the big empty cavern where the audience would sit. There in the front row, just as she had promised, sat Miranda's mother, smiling and nodding toward her daughter.

The music filtered softly onto the stage. The music that usually filled Miranda with a lightness that lifted her in magic gliding movement now filled her with a strange sadness. It was the sadness of the dark eyes that had watched other children dancing, the dark eyes that now watched Miranda dance. Heavy, aching sadness poured into Miranda.

Tap, tap, tap. The teacher's cane marked Miranda's missed cue. *Tap, tap, tap.* The cane prodded her forward into the spotlight. Miranda moved to the music automatically, the steps paired to the rhythm of the music from hours of practice. But her spins wobbled with the heavy sadness. She strained to leap, her legs thick with the sadness the music pulsed into her. She didn't look at her mother in the audience. She couldn't look at those dark eyes watching her dance across the stage. And the sadness stopped only when the music ended and the curtain pulled across the stage.

Mrs. Sommers approached the group, "I know that dancing on a big stage thinking about all the people who will be watching you can make you feel a little shaky and unsure. But, remember the picture I told you to keep in your mind. Just concentrate on that, and we'll keep practicing here today until it feels just like we're back in our own little studio." She looked at Miranda, "Just let the music guide you and you'll be fine. Now take a fifteen-minute break, and we'll try it again."

Miranda's mother was waiting for her as she walked down to take a seat. Mrs. Montero put her arm around her daughter.

"Your teacher seems to think that you all had a little stage fright. Did you feel nervous up there, *m'ija?*"

"I guess so," Miranda whispered, looking away.

"You know, you didn't look scared to me, Miranda. I'm used to seeing you so happy flying across the floor, but this time you just looked so sad, like something was weighing you down. What is it, *m'ija?*"

Miranda's eyes were filling with tears when she looked up at her mother. "I heard you talking to the teacher about when you were a little girl."

Mrs. Montero put her arms around Miranda. "*Ay, m'ija,*" she whispered as she kissed her daughter on the top of her head. She held her a moment then knelt down to look into her daughter's face. "Miranda, you only heard the first part of the conversation, and not the most important part. I told your teacher not to feel embarrassed or upset. You see, Miranda, when I watch you dance and see how free and happy you are floating with the music, I feel free and light myself. It's hard to explain, but seeing you is more beautiful to me than all my childhood daydreams. And when you leap and leave the ground, I feel this wonderful lightness inside me. It's your gift, Miranda, but it's also a gift to all of us who watch you."

Miranda looked up at her mother's eyes, her

mother's dark, happy, dancing eyes, and the sadness lifted away from them both as they stood there with their arms around each other.

Tap, tap, tap. Mrs. Sommers called Miranda's group back onto the stage. Miranda grazed her mother's cheek with a quick kiss and dashed up the stairs, savoring the new lightness that lifted her so easily forward onto the stage. *Tap, tap, tap.* They all took their places. *Tap, tap, tap.* The Music Center was silent.

Then the music began, weaving its magic through Miranda. She felt the rhythm build with every breath. The strong, electric rhythm pulsed through her. It drew her forward, spinning to the front of the stage. Miranda looked up and met her mother's smiling face, her dark and shining eyes. And then the music lifted them both into the air, soaring them across the stage, Miranda and the girl with the dancing dark eyes.

Tía Luisa

Julio rolled over on his side and pulled the royal blue comforter over his head to block out the morning sun. As he turned, he felt his stomach do a somersault, and a queasy feeling bubbled up to his throat.

"Oooh," he groaned as he felt his stomach quivering like the squares of red and orange Jell-O in the school cafeteria. The thought of jiggling Jell-O made his stomach feel even shakier, so he quickly put the picture out of his mind.

Just at that moment his mom entered the room.

"Good morning," his mother called out in a cheery voice as she noticed the lump under the blankets. "Come on out of hiding. You're running a little late," she continued, smiling as she walked toward his bed.

She lifted and peeked under the comforter. Her smile disappeared immediately when she uncovered Julio's face. His forehead was wrinkled and his eyes were squinting from the pain.

"*Ay, m'ijo,*" his mother exclaimed, "what's the matter?"

"Oooh," groaned Julio again. "My stomach, it feels all shaky and terrible." His head felt heavy, and his muscles felt a little sore as he pushed himself up to a sitting position. "My head doesn't feel very good either," he declared as his mother leaned forward and placed her hand on his forehead.

"You feel like you might have a slight fever. Lie down again, *m'ijo*, while I take your temperature," his mother said in a serious tone.

Julio snuggled back under the comforter while his mother left to get the thermometer from the bathroom medicine cabinet. His head felt better resting on his soft, white pillow. But his stomach kept making flip-flops as he lay there staring at the ceiling.

Julio's mother returned and gently tucked the new plastic digital thermometer under his tongue. He didn't feel like having anything in his mouth with that bubbly feeling in his throat. "At least," he thought, "this is quicker than the old glass thermometer we used to use."

Beep, beep, beep. Julio's mother removed the thermometer as the tiny alarm rang out.

"That's good," said his mother with a sigh. "It's just one degree above normal. It looks like your body's fighting the flu."

"Great," grumbled Julio as he pulled the blankets over his head again. "At least if I'm asleep," he thought, "I won't know how miserable I really am."

"That's good; get some more rest. I'll close the blinds and shut off the hall light so you don't have to tunnel under the blankets like a gopher."

As soon as the room began to darken, Julio

pushed out from under the blankets. He could hardly believe he was lying still in his bed. He felt like he was in a rowboat, his stomach sloshing to and fro with the waves. His body felt tired and heavy, so he quickly drifted off to sleep and into a dream. In the dream, he was in a hospital in a big room with a high white ceiling and bright lights. A woman in a white uniform entered the room pushing a big machine made out of grey metal. She rolled the machine up to Julio and pressed the cold metal against his stomach. It began to make clicking and whirring sounds and sent a picture to a TV screen across the room. There inside of Julio's stomach were two goldfish, swimming around and around in circles. The nurse looked at the screen, shook her head, and left the room. In just a few seconds, she was back carrying what looked like a large white basketball.

"Here, just swallow this and you'll feel much better," she said. "Open wide," she continued as she tossed the giant pill toward Julio. Julio opened his mouth as wide as he could as the huge white ball came sailing toward him. Just as it reached his face, Julio woke up with a start.

When he opened his eyes, he was relieved to see that he was back in his bedroom again. But there, at the foot of his bed, stood a lady wearing a stiff white apron. For a second, Julio froze, afraid the woman in the white uniform had followed him out of his dream.

"Hello, *m'ijito*," the woman called to him. "I

heard you were sick, so I came by to help make you feel better."

Julio cringed at her words. "That's okay," Julio responded. "I just need to get some pink medicine from the doctor."

Just at that moment, his mother came in the door and stood beside the woman. "Julio, you remember *Tía* Luisa. She was at your *abuelos'* house when I called and told them you were sick. She came right over to see how she could help."

Tía Luisa smiled and playfully patted the lump in the blankets that was Julio's right foot.

"I'm fixing just what you need." Then she turned toward Julio's mother. "I'd better check on *el pollo*."

"I'll help you," replied Julio's mother.

"No, no, *no te preocupes*. You stay here, *con el paciente*." *Tía* Luisa winked at Julio and left the room.

"Mom, is she a nurse?" Julio asked in a slightly shaky voice when he figured *Tía* Luisa was back in the kitchen.

"No, *m'ijo*, but she learned how to take care of people when they get sick from her mother. Her mother was a *curandera* in Mexico. It's sort of like a nurse, but they use herbs and other natural things for cures."

"And she's my *tía?*" asked Julio.

"Everyone calls her *Tía* Luisa. Your *abuela* has been friends with her ever since they were little girls. She's just been part of our family for as long as I can remember," replied his mother.

Julio responded with another groan as his stomach did a sudden cartwheel. Julio's mother wrinkled up her forehead. Little lines appeared around her eyes as she watched Julio wrap his arms across his stomach. "I think I'll give the doctor a call and see what he thinks we should do for you," she said, sharing her thoughts out loud.

"Great!" responded Julio as quickly as he could. He was relieved that Dr. Martin would be the one deciding what medicine he should take.

Julio didn't want to go back to sleep. He was worried that his dream would return. Instead, he reached over to the bookcase on the left side of his bed and snatched an *X-Men* comic book off a shelf. He propped his pillow against the wall and leaned against it in a half-sitting, half-lying position.

Just then his older brother entered the room.

"Hey, squirt, hurry up. You're going to miss your soccer practice," snapped ten-year-old Eddie. He hesitated as his brother put down the comic book that was covering his face. "Boy, your face looks green enough to be in the comics!"

"Thanks," replied Julio, "that makes me feel a whole lot better. Oooh, my stomach," he groaned as he tried to sit up straighter.

Eddie looked at his little brother struggling in the bed. He thought about what he had said. "I'm sorry. I didn't know you felt so bad." Eddie hesitated. "So that's why *Tía* Luisa is here," he said as though he had solved an important mystery.

"Yeah, mom says she's a *cura—cura*—something. She helps cure people," interrupted Julio.

"Ummm. *That's* why she's doing all that stuff in the kitchen," Eddie muttered.

"What stuff?" Julio shot back immediately, his voice rising.

"You know, boiling chicken and stuff," replied Eddie.

"What's the big deal about boiling chicken?" smirked Julio.

"Don't you know what they do with chickens?" Eddie responded with surprise in his voice. He edged closer to his eight-year-old brother. "They boil all the fat out of them. Then they take the hot chicken fat and rub it all over the sick person's body."

Julio's stomach made more Jell-O-like bounces as he pictured *Tía* Luisa entering his room with a bowl of hot chicken fat.

"And they carry potions around in little bags that make people do weird things," added Eddie.

"How do *you* know?" Julio demanded.

"Lalo and Nena told me about it. And they heard that *Tía* Luisa has these magical cards in her purse that she uses to decide whether the person's going to get better or die," continued Eddie.

Julio's eyes got wider and wider as Eddie spoke. "Tell mom to come here," Julio pleaded. "Tell her I need her right away!"

Eddie heard the fright in his little brother's

voice. "Okay, okay, I'll get her," he replied, dashing out of the room.

In a couple of minutes Julio's mother rushed into the bedroom. "Julio, what's the matter? Your brother said you were feeling worse," she said as she sat next to him and put her arm around his shoulders.

"I just wanted you to ask the doctor for the pink medicine. It'll make me feel better, and then I won't need anything else," suggested Julio.

"I just talked with Dr. Martin. He said it sounds like the flu that's going around. The pink medicine won't help. He said you just need to rest and try some clear chicken soup and some chamomile tea with toast to settle your stomach," Julio's mother explained.

"And what about *Tía* Luisa?" asked Julio.

"Oh, she's been preparing things for you all morning . . . And here she is," announced Julio's mother as *Tía* Luisa entered the bedroom carrying a tray.

Julio stopped breathing for a moment as he looked at the large bowl sitting on the tray that *Tía* Luisa carried towards him. She set the tray down on the top of the night stand to the right of his bed. The yellow liquid in the bowl made swirling motions as the tray came to rest. *Tía* Luisa reached into her apron pocket and pulled out a small square packet. It was made of soft white paper. Julio could see that there was a dark powder inside of it. She dropped the packet into a cup of hot water on the tray.

Julio felt his heart beat a little faster and began to take short, quick breaths as he pictured *Tía* Luisa pouring the hot yellow liquid in the bowl all over him and forcing the cup of the dark potion down his throat.

Julio turned quickly toward his mother and blurted out, "I thought we were going to do what the doctor said."

"That's what's so amazing," exclaimed his mother. "Just look at what *Tía* Luisa had already made for you—chicken soup and toast!"

"What about the potion she put into the cup?" pleaded Julio.

"You mean the *te de manzanilla,*" answered *Tía* Luisa.

"*Manzanilla* is the Spanish word for chamomile," his mother explained. "Dr. Martin and *Tía* Luisa came up with the same cure."

"*Todo está muy caliente.* Everything's too hot right now," added *Tía* Luisa. "So I brought something for us to do while we wait for it all to cool down."

Tía Luisa sat down on the corner of Julio's bed. She pulled a large deck of cards with gold and black designs out of the other apron pocket.

Julio felt his face get very hot. "That's okay. I can just sit here and read my comic book," he replied.

But *Tía* Luisa had already begun placing cards in front of both of them. She counted out loud,

"*Uno, dos, tres, cuatro . . .*" until they each had seven cards in front of them. Julio stared at his cards, wondering what they would say was going to happen to him.

"Pick up you cards, *m'ijo*," urged *Tía* Luisa.

"Uh, uh . . ." Julio hesitated. "I'll wait for you."

"Okay, then," she replied and placed the remaining cards in a stack between them. Then she lifted her palm above the deck.

Julio wanted to put his hands over his ears so he wouldn't hear the magic words she would say over the cards. But before he could lift his hands, *Tía* Luisa lowered her hand and spread the cards across the bed. Julio felt a quiver vibrate from his stomach up through his chest forming a big knot in his throat.

Then *Tía* Luisa looked up at Julio, smiled and said, "Go fish!"

Julio froze for a few seconds, and then a tickle began in the pit of his stomach. It tickled its way up past his chest. It untied the knot in his throat and burst out as Julio began to laugh.

Julio's mother and *Tía* Luisa gave each other puzzled looks.

"Go fish," Julio repeated. Julio held onto his stomach. He laughed, then he groaned, then he laughed again.

MARI, MARI, *MARIPOSA*

Mari stood straight and still, trying to blend in with the trees around her. Only the wisps of her brown, wavy hair that flowed down her back moved slightly in the breeze. She spread her arms out at her sides, balanced in mid-air like thin, leafless branches.

Mari smiled as the butterfly's tiny legs tickled their way up her arm. The butterfly dipped the velvet black edges of its bright yellow wings up and down as it danced its way towards the other butterflies that rested on her shoulders and chest. Two orange fritillary butterflies opened and closed their wings like miniature painted fans as they held their places on the brightly colored flowers printed on Mari's blouse.

Mari had crept up silently on each one and with one quick swipe had caught them in her soft, flowing butterfly net. Then she had reached in carefully and grazed her fingers gently across their wings a few times. The bright, silky powder from the butterflies' wings made the tips of her fingers feel soft and slick. Slowly she had eased her hand under their legs, and, with them sitting in her cupped hand, pulled them out of the net. The butterflies fluttered their wings, but they could only

glide across her hand and onto her arm. Mari had taken off just enough powder to keep them from flying away.

One of the orange butterflies had managed a little leap onto her blouse and crawled toward her face. Mari had lifted the other one onto her shoulder where it spread its wings to feel the warm sun while the other explored this strange new human tree. But the yellow swallowtail was the largest and most beautiful butterfly she had ever caught. Its four-inch wings looped in graceful yellow and black arcs across its shiny black body. It flapped its wings open and shut over and over again as it tried to lift itself off Mari's arm. But those delicate wings that had always let it sail so quickly and easily through the air just made it slip faster across Mari's arm. Mari saw the butterfly struggling, and so with her other hand, she carefully boosted it up to her shoulder to rest.

As the butterflies took little journeys across her shoulders and the front of her blouse, Mari snapped off small branches of flowers to take home for the aquarium that would be the butterflies' new home.

"They'll rest on the branches and drink the nectar from the flowers," she thought. Then she piled the cuttings into a mixed bouquet of different colors and sweet smells and dropped them into the butterfly net. She tossed the handle of the butterfly net over her left shoulder as she marched out of the small cluster of trees and flowering bushes in her yard towards the screen porch in the rear of the house.

Her eleven-year-old brother, Antonio, was kneeling on the ground tightening the sprockets on his blue ten-speed bike. He looked up as he heard the footsteps approaching. There stood Mari, the brightly colored flowers on her blouse and the yellow and orange butterflies glowing in the afternoon sun.

"What'd ya do, stick pins through 'em to keep them on your blouse?" asked Antonio with a sneer.

"How could you even think of saying anything so gruesome? I never hurt *any* living thing," Mari snapped back. "It's magic. Just watch. They'll even dance with me."

Mari spread her arms and took three gentle turns around the edge of the steps. The butterflies fluttered their wings as she spun. Their delicate butterfly feet took tiny dance steps as the spinning movement rocked them back and forth.

"Mari, Mari, *Mari-posa,*" sang Mari as she twirled right up to the porch.

Antonio looked in amazement at his sister. He hadn't been serious about the pins. He knew his sister wouldn't even kill the ants that invaded the kitchen in small armies every now and then.

"How do you get them to stay on you like that?" asked Antonio.

"I told you. I have special powers that make them stick to me like a magnet."

"Come on, get real. Tell me what you did to them," Antonio insisted. He was sure his sister had no magical powers, but was curious to learn how she could have pulled off such a trick.

"It's easy," Mari replied rolling her eyes at him. "I just rub a little powder off their wings and then they can't fly away."

"*And,* Miss Bug-Lover, how are they supposed to eat and stay alive? Those aren't real flowers on your blouse, you know," quipped Antonio.

"I know what I'm doing," Mari fired the words back at him quickly. "I'm going to put them in my old aquarium with some flowers I picked."

Antonio stood up and faced Mari.

"I hate to tell you, but I don't think a few flowers in a little aquarium can keep them alive for long."

"Then I'll take them outside and put them back in the garden," replied Mari.

"Yeah, and because they can't fly anymore, they'll be easy targets for hungry birds," said Antonio, shaking his head.

Mari's smile disappeared. She wrinkled her forehead and a serious look came across her face. She no longer felt warm and happy inside as she had when she danced with the butterflies on her shoulders. Suddenly she felt sad and worried.

"I never meant to hurt them, Antonio. Do you think the powder will come back?" Mari asked hopefully.

Antonio just shrugged his shoulders and went

back to fixing his bike.

Mari thought for a moment. "I'll just have to take you back and stay with you to protect you while you eat," she whispered to the butterflies. Antonio was facing away from her now. He didn't even notice Mari turn and walk back into the garden.

Mari lifted the butterflies one at a time and placed them in the middle of clusters of flowers. Then she took her position as a human scarecrow in front of the flower bushes, ready to charge and scare away any birds. A small brown speckled sparrow entered the garden and skipped across the top branches of a nearby bush. Mari ran towards the sparrow, waving her arms and making catlike hissing sounds. The sparrow shot upward and out of the garden immediately. Mari watched the bird dart away from her. She was glad the butterflies were safe. But she was upset that the sparrows she usually watched play in the bushes would now have to become afraid of her.

Just then, two black birds with shiny feathers and yellow eyes swooped down onto the ground in front of the flower bushes. Mari made big stomping steps towards the birds, and they lifted off the ground together.

Mari looked for the butterflies in the bushes to make sure the birds had not snatched one on their way into the garden. The butterflies were still sitting in the middle of the flower bushes. But, instead of drinking the nectar as Mari had expected them to do, they had spread their wings and were warming themselves in the sun.

Mari heard some rustling above her and looked up. There, huddled together on the telephone wire leading to the house, were four ravens. Their thick, strong claws held them firmly in place as they leaned their heads forward to look down on Mari and the garden below. Mari had always felt a little frightened of the ravens. They stood almost eighteen inches high, with bulky, dark bodies, pointed black beaks, and dark shadowy eyes that seemed to follow you as you moved. And they always came in small groups, announcing themselves in hoarse, ugly cries that scared away the smaller birds.

Mari froze, shielding the butterflies with her body. She was afraid to yell or throw something at them. She was worried she might miss and pictured the four diving down from the wire with their sharp beaks pointed straight at her.

The birds cocked their heads and stared at Mari. Mari started to take another step backward when the quiet garden was rocked by the sound of two loud backfires on the other side of the fence. Startled by the unexpected noise, Mari jumped in place. The noise had frightened the ravens too, and they leapt off the wires together, complaining in loud *caws* as they flew away.

The hum of a motor now filtered across the fence. Mari knew the familiar sound. It was Mr. Sanders's old gasoline lawn mower. Her parents always complained that it was noisy and polluted the air, but today Mari was glad Mr. Sanders had not traded it in for the new, quieter models.

She looked at her butterflies. The noise and threat of the ravens had not bothered them. Mari was glad they were enjoying the sun on their outspread wings, but was concerned that they hadn't tried to drink any nectar from the flowers that surrounded them.

"This isn't going to work," thought Mari. But she wasn't sure what to do. It might be hours before the butterflies decided to eat. And even then, how would she know when they had drunk enough nectar? She couldn't stay and protect them all afternoon, especially on school days. She thought about taking them to the vet. She knew he took care of other animal besides cats and dogs. She had seen a snake and a bird in his office, but no one ever brought insects to the vet.

"I'll bet there are scientists who study butterflies," she thought. But she didn't know any scientists, much less one who studied only butterflies.

Then she remembered Mrs. Torres. Mrs. Torres, the science teacher at the high school, lived only two doors down. Mari wasn't sure she knew how to take care of live animals, since she heard that her classes cut up dead frogs. But, Mari didn't know where else to go. So, she gently lifted the butterflies off the flower bush, settled them on her shoulders, and walked off towards Mrs. Torres's house.

Mari walked up the driveway to the bright yellow house with white trim and stood on the welcome mat. As she looked at the doorbell, she realized that even though Mrs. Torres and her mother were friends, she had never really talked with Mrs. Torres before. They had said hello when they saw each other on the block and once or twice at the grocery store. And Mari had said "Thank you" on Halloween when she dropped caramels and pennies into her shopping bag.

Mari took a deep breath, scooted the wandering butterflies back up to her shoulders, and rang the doorbell. She felt relieved when Mrs. Torres opened the door holding a long-haired black cat with white-mitten paws and a white patch on its chest.

"Oh, my goodness," laughed Mrs. Torres looking at Mari. "Here's a walking garden, butterflies and all." Her shiny dark eyes and warm smile were so friendly that Mari knew she had come to the right place.

"I need to talk to you about my butterflies, Mrs. Torres. I don't know what to do to take care of them," Mari began.

"Come on in, Mari, and let's see what we can figure out. But first, tell me how you ever got them to just sit there on your shoulders."

Mrs. Torres had meant what she said as a compliment to Mari. She expected Mari to smile back and share her secret. Instead, Mari's face became very serious, and she looked away from Mrs. Torres as she entered the house. She turned toward Mrs. Torres when she heard the door click shut, but looked down at her feet as she spoke.

"I'm afraid that I've done something really bad to the butterflies. I didn't mean to hurt them, but I rubbed the powder off their wings and now they can't fly around and find their food. They're going to die, and it's all my fault." Mari tightened her jaw and bit down hard to hold back the tears that were beginning to well in her eyes. She was ready to be scolded. She thought she deserved it.

But, instead, Mrs. Torres cupped her chin in her right hand and lifted her face so their eyes could meet. Mari was surprised by Mrs. Torres's friendly, smiling eyes.

"Mari, you haven't hurt them at all. They even seem content, sitting there so calmly and peacefully on your shoulders. We just have to figure out what is the best way to take care of domesticated butterflies," said Mrs. Torres.

"No, these are fritillary, and this yellow one is a swallowtail," responded Mari pointing to each.

Mrs. Torres laughed. "By *domesticated,* I mean tame instead of wild butterflies. Just like my cat Tyler here is a domesticated cat, and a lion is a wild cat," explained Mrs. Torres, setting the cat on the floor.

"But they don't make cans of butterfly food like they make cat food," replied Mari. "And I tried to let them feed in the bushes while I watched them, but it would take hours."

"You're right, and you can't hand-feed a butterfly like you can a kitten or a puppy. They need to be able to find food on their own," agreed Mrs. Torres.

"But then the birds will eat them. You should have seen the ravens just waiting to get them," added Mari.

"Hmmmm." Mrs. Torres hesitated. "I think I have a solution. Follow me."

Mari followed Mrs. Torres down the hall and through her bright yellow kitchen, out the back door, and into the yard. Two more cats were sunning themselves on benches in the patio. They walked past two rabbit hutches with big, brown, lop-eared rabbits peering out at them.

"I didn't know you had so many animals," exclaimed Mari.

"Oh yes, and I have two chinchillas and a green Amazon parrot inside," replied Mrs. Torres. "Before I became a science teacher, I seriously considered becoming a veterinarian."

"Why didn't you?" asked Mari.

"Because as much as I love animals, I decided I liked kids better," Mrs. Torres responded.

They had reached the very back of the yard. There in one corner was a small house made completely out of squares of glass.

"This is an old greenhouse that was here when we bought the house. I've been meaning to fix it up and start growing different kinds of plants in it.

I've been so busy that I haven't had time to go to the nursery to buy them." Mrs. Torres smiled at Mari. " Now I'll have a good reason."

Mrs. Torres opened the door, and they stepped inside.

"There are a few plants and flowers," continued Mrs. Torres, "but we'll need many more."

"I'll ask my mom and bring some from our garden," suggested Mari.

"Great! There are plenty of empty pots here to plant them in. Why don't we leave your friends here on the flowers while you get the plants from your garden and I make a quick trip to the nursery? We can meet back here in, let's say, an hour and a half."

Mari felt happy, relieved, and excited all at the same time.

"It's perfect," she said as she lifted the butterflies onto the blossoms. "They'll have food and sunlight and space and be completely protected."

"And we'll talk about when you can come and visit them. They're in my greenhouse, but they're still your butterflies," Mrs. Torres emphasized.

Mari was quiet for a moment. "I guess no one really owns butterflies. But, thanks, I would like to visit them whenever I can."

They closed the door as the butterflies danced in little flutters across the bright bouquets of potted flowers.

"Do you like other insects too, Mari?" asked Mrs. Torres as they walked back into the house.

"Well, some I guess," replied Mari thoughtfully. "I like ladybugs, both the shiny red ones and the spotted ones. In the summer I catch June beetles just for a second to feel them buzz in my hands, and then I let them fly away. And I like dragonflies with fairy wings and cochinillas that tickle your hand and roll up into a little ball, and—"

"I guess you answered my question," interrupted Mrs. Torres. "But do you know what job each one of those insects do?"

"Job?" repeated Mari.

"Sure, each insect has a special job to do. For example, ladybugs eat aphids—tiny green bugs that destroy roses and other plants. Dragonflies help us by eating mosquito larvae so that there are fewer mosquitoes to bite us. And even your little cochinillas help break up the soil to keep it breathing. Your butterflies help take pollen on their feet and bodies from one plant to another." Mrs. Torres was concerned that she was starting to sound too much like a teacher, so decided to stop there.

"I never really thought about them *do*ing anything, except maybe eating and flying or crawling around," Mari responded.

"You know," added Mrs. Torres, "you might even think about becoming an entomologist one day."

Mari gave Mrs. Torres a puzzled look. They were in the entryway now, by a small telephone table. Mrs. Torres picked up a pencil and wrote the long word in big letters on a memo pad.

"En-to-mo-lo-gist." She read each syllable as she wrote. "It means someone who studies insects," she explained as she tore off the sheet and handed it to Mari.

Mari took the paper and studied the letters. "En-to-*mo*-lo-gist," she repeated slowly, then faster, "Entomologist!"

"That's right. It's just something to think about," said Mrs. Torres as she walked Mari to the front door. "Okay, I'll see you here about two o'clock."

Mari waved goodbye to Mrs. Torres and Tyler, who stood at the door as she walked down the porch steps. She stopped for a moment at the foot of the stairs when she heard the door click shut and studied the long word on the sheet of paper. Mari smiled and lifted her head high.

"Mari, Mari, Entomologist," she sang as she skipped down the driveway.

THE VISITORS

It was two in the morning, and the only sound in the Ríos family's house was the *click-click, tap-tap* of Mrs. Ríos's fingers working in the den on the computer keyboard. She yawned and stretched as she heard the clock chiming down the hall. She hit a few more keys to save her work and then flipped off the computer. It was so quiet that she heard her tennis shoes make faint squeaking sounds as she walked across the shiny hardwood floor to turn off the light.

Suddenly there was a rattling sound, and then a loud *thud* from the patio just the other side of the den door. Startled, Mrs. Ríos let out a quick gasp. She covered her mouth and listened. Soft scratching and crunching noises filtered into the silent room. Mrs. Ríos took a deep breath and tip-toed up to the sliding glass door.

"It's okay—the door's locked and has a bar across it," she said to herself as she parted a small space between the drapes, just big enough to peep out with one eye onto the patio. She scanned across the patio table and benches, the flower pots, and the gardening cart. Everything looked like it always did except for the metal dog feeder, which was lying on its side. She opened the space in the drapes a little more to get a better look. At first she only saw a tail. The tail was hanging out of the metal feeder. It was long, thin, grayish-pink, and hairless. She could hear whatever creature it was rummaging inside the feeder.

No longer worried it might be a prowler, Mrs. Ríos pushed the drapes apart. In the quiet of the night, the sound of the sliding drapes filled the room and filtered out onto the patio. The crunching came to a sudden stop, and a pale grey, furry creature sat up in the feed box and turned its head toward the sliding door. Mrs. Ríos froze for a moment and stared at its beady eyes that glowed red in the patio lights and its pointed snout framed with spiky white teeth.

"That's the biggest rat I've ever seen in my whole *life,*" she thought to herself. She figured it was as big as their calico cat, who was safely sleeping in her basket in the laundry room. "And where are our *guard* dogs?" she thought. "Nice and cozy asleep in their dog houses, no doubt."

Mrs. Ríos realized it was up to her to take care of the intruder. So, she took a deep breath and began to pound with her open palms on the sliding glass door, repeating, "Shoo! Shoo!" as she did. The creature stared at her for a moment, gave her a bored look, then climbed farther into the feeder and continued its free evening meal. Mrs. Ríos pounded even harder, but the creature was too busy making its own crunching noises in the feeder to even notice.

Mrs. Ríos stopped pounding and considered what she could do. She could get the broom from the kitchen and chase it out of the patio, but this was a rat that didn't frighten easily. There was no telling what it might do. She could wake up her husband and the dogs to help her, but she didn't want to disturb the household over a few servings of dry dogfood. So, she watched as the tail disappeared deeper into the feeder, then she closed the drapes and left the room. Slipping under the blankets on her bed, she could hear the metal feeder rattle every now and then as she closed her eyes and drifted off to sleep.

The next morning at the breakfast table, Mrs. Ríos told her husband and two sons about the early morning visitor.

"*How* big did you say it was, Mom?" ten-year-old Sergio asked, looking at his mother with wide curious eyes.

"It was as big as Pepper the cat and had an ugly bald tail almost as long as hers," she replied.

"You must be exaggerating a little or maybe you couldn't see it so well in the dark. We have field mice, but no big rats around here," her husband declared.

"Look, I know what I saw. The crazy creature sat up and stared right at me, like it was daring me to do something," she insisted as she picked up the empty cereal bowls to clear the kitchen table. "It had these teeth like little daggers sticking out of its long snout. I'm worried it could bite someone or find its way into the house. What are we going to do about it?"

Sergio gave his younger brother Rudy a quick look and a nod of his head, then interrupted: "We're done. Can Rudy and I go watch Saturday cartoons now?"

"Sure," their parents replied at the same time.

Their father stood up and began helping clear the table. They could hear him making suggestions as they left the room.

"We could lock the dogs out of the side runs and leave them in the patio at night instead," Mr. Ríos began.

"Come on, Rudy, we've got some plans to make," Sergio said, grabbing his little brother by the arm.

Six-year-old Rudy gave his older brother a puzzled look as he followed along into the front room.

"What are you talking about?" Rudy asked as they entered the room.

"We've got to figure out a way to capture it ourselves," Sergio replied.

"How?" said a surprised, but interested, Rudy.

"I'm not sure, but maybe we could take the netting off our soccer goal and use some ropes to drop it on him," Sergio suggested.

"Yeah, we could shoot the ropes with lasers and the net would fall and catch him!" Rudy added.

Sergio just shook his head. He remembered he was talking to a six-year-old whose ideas came from watching cartoons and reading super-hero comic books.

"I'll let you know how you can help, Rudy. Now just turn on the TV, " Sergio replied, settling on the couch in his usual Saturday morning cartoon-watching position.

They had watched cartoons for about twenty minutes when they heard their father yelling into the house from the side door: "Everybody, come here quick!"

Mrs. Ríos and the two boys dashed down the hallway and across the kitchen to the doorway.

"Come on out and look. The dogs took care of our mysterious bandit," Mr. Ríos announced.

"That's it. That's the creature," Mrs. Ríos exclaimed as the three of them stepped into the dog run and saw the grey furry animal lying on its side near one of the dog houses.

"It must have tried to leave through the run and the dogs got it," Mr. Ríos suggested.

"Are the dogs all right?" asked Mrs. Ríos.

"Sure, the poor thing probably didn't even put up a fight. You see, it's not a rat; it's an opossum. When they get trapped, they freeze and play dead. Sometimes it works, but other times, well . . ." Mr. Ríos just shook his head.

"Are you sure it's not just *playing* dead now, Dad?" asked Sergio hopefully.

"No, son. I checked. He's not pretending. I'm afraid there's nothing we can do."

"Look at that weird tail," observed Rudy.

"Yes, they hang by their tails, *m'ijo*," his father explained. "They wrap it around a tree branch and hang upside down."

Sergio and Rudy felt sad that the creature was dead, but it did make them feel safer when they came up for a closer look at the jagged row of sharp teeth.

"The dogs must have been scared, too, when they saw his teeth," said Rudy. He wanted to find a reason why his dogs would hurt a creature that was trying to play dead.

"They're trained to protect us all from anything that might hurt us. They were just trying to do their job," Mr. Ríos explained.

The two boys watched their father lift the stiff, lifeless opossum into a plastic trash bag. They waved goodbye to him as their father drove off in his pickup truck.

For a short time, the sight of the opossum lying so still on its side kept coming into the boys' minds. But after a while, it began to feel like any other Saturday afternoon. It was only when they set up the soccer goal on the lawn that Sergio thought about his plans to capture the creature alive.

About eight that evening, Sergio and Rudy entered their bedroom to change into their pajamas. All of a sudden, they heard the dogs barking and growling and the side door slam as their father went out to calm them down. In a few minutes, Mr. Ríos called to his family again, "Come to the dog-run quick, everybody. Come see what the dogs found."

Sergio and Rudy looked at each other.

"Oh, no, not again," whispered Sergio.

The hall seemed longer this time as they walked toward the side door. They tried not to think about what they might see once they stepped out of the house. When they entered the side run, they saw their father and mother standing in front of one of the dog houses smiling. Mr. Ríos motioned for them to come closer.

"I have a happy surprise for you this time, boys. Look what the dogs found in the dog house."

The two boys got down on their knees and peered into the dog house through the wide opening in the front. There, far back in a corner of the dog house, was a tiny version of the opossum they had seen earlier that day. As they stuck their heads in farther for a closer look, the baby opossum scooted farther into the corner, opened its narrow, tooth-filled mouth, and let out a big hiss. The two boys bumped heads as they rushed to pull their faces away quickly. "Ow," they cried together as they rubbed their heads and stood up.

"It's not very friendly," complained Sergio.

"Yeah," added Rudy. "It just *spit* on us."

"No it didn't," corrected Sergio, "it just hissed."

"It's probably really scared right now. The dogs killed its mother and then it got chased and barked at. Finally, it sees you boys coming towards it in a place where it's trapped and can't get away,"

Mr. Ríos explained.

"Can we keep him, can we, please? He doesn't have a mother to take care of him, and next time the dogs might kill him," pleaded Sergio.

"I don't know," replied Mrs. Ríos. "It *is* a wild animal."

"Your mom's right. You can't expect the opossum to be like a cat or even a rabbit. They're not meant to be pets."

"We know," said Rudy, "but it's a baby and needs our help now."

"We could take care of it for a while and see if maybe it'll learn not to be so scared," added Sergio.

"Okay, I'll tell you what. I'll put the opossum in our old rabbit hutch. You boys will be in charge of its food and water until it's big enough to take of itself and be free. Is it a deal?" their father asked.

"It's a deal," shouted the boys at the same time.

Their father took off his blue and grey flannel shirt. He got on his hands and knees and crept into the opening of the dog house. Quickly he flung his shirt over the rigid, hissing little opossum. He rolled the shirt into a pouch and lifted the creature out of the dog house. He took long, swift steps over to the old rabbit hutch, lifted the roof, and gently placed the little bundle on the hutch floor. Mr. Ríos slowly lifted his shirt away from the opossum until it was free. He pulled out his shirt and quietly put the hutch roof down.

"There," said Mr. Ríos, "he's nice and safe for

now."

"He?" replied Sergio.

"I can't be sure, but I think so. Anyway, I'm not sure that matters at this point."

Sergio and Rudy tried to see the opossum through the wire mesh front, but the patio light didn't reflect enough to see clearly into the back corner. What they would have seen was the opossum sitting motionless with his mouth open wide, showing his row of sharp, pointed teeth to anyone who might come near.

"You can see it tomorrow. He's had a pretty upsetting night and needs to be left alone for a while," their mother said as she put her hands on their shoulders and nudged them toward the house.

"What are we going to name our new pet?" Rudy asked his brother as they entered the house.

Before Sergio could reply, his mother quickly interrupted, "Wait a minute, boys. Your father and I never said this was going to be a pet. We're taking care of and protecting him right now, because he's a helpless baby, but that doesn't mean we're going to keep him. We'll have to do what's best for the creature."

"Maybe he'll like living here with us and want to stay," Sergio added.

"Maybe so, but you can't count on that," his mother replied.

"Couldn't we just give him a name until then?" Rudy pleaded.

"I guess even temporary guests have names. Okay, but remember what I said," his mother warned.

"Sure, Mom, sure," Rudy replied as Sergio shook his head in agreement.

Mrs. Ríos heard the boys trying out different names as they moved down the hall together towards their bedroom.

"How about Fang?" suggested Rudy.

"You've got to be kidding!" shot back Sergio, shaking his head as they entered the bedroom and closed the door.

The next morning they went out to the hutch to check on their new little guest. Their parents had told them that opossums sleep during the day, so they were careful not to make too much noise. They lifted the hutch roof quietly and put in one of Pepper's old ceramic water dishes and a handful of dogfood in an empty tuna can. Then they tip-toed away to get dressed for church and the drive to their *abuelos'* house for lunch.

The little opossum slept curled up in the corner the whole day while the Ríos family was gone. The dogs came up to the hutch and pressed their noses against the wire mesh to catch the scent they had tracked the night before. They barked a few times, but the little opossum just curled up tighter and stayed in the dark corner.

It was twilight when the Ríos family pulled up into the driveway in their red four-by-four. Mr. Ríos had barely shifted into park when the boys threw open the doors and darted across the yard to the side gate. Sergio flipped the lock and the boys barreled down the dog-run straight to the rabbit hutch.

"Hi, Bravo." Rudy called out the name that the boys and their cousins had decided on that afternoon at the *abuelos'* house. It was a perfect name. It meant wild and fierce, but it could also mean brave, which they hoped he would be eventually.

The opossum had been squinting through the wire mesh, surveying the patio and the yard. When the boys approached the hutch, he began to move backwards. By the time they lifted the lid, he was back in the far corner. Sergio reached in and dropped some pieces of *papas fritas* and carrots left over from lunch onto the wire floor. The opossum opened his mouth and showed his teeth when he saw the hand reach into the cage. Rudy looked at the row of teeth, white, jagged, and sharp as needles. He decided to toss the pieces of bread he had brought the opossum into the cage rather than put in his hand.

Sergio looked down at the dogfood they had left that morning. A few were knocked out of the tuna can, but almost all the food was still there.

"He didn't even eat the dog food we left him," said Sergio in a worried tone.

Sergio put the roof down gently and walked over to the tool and gardening cart across the patio. He grabbed his father's leather work gloves and pulled them on as he walked back to the hutch.

"What are you going to do?" Rudy asked, feeling a little worried.

"We've got to get him to eat something or he'll die," Sergio insisted. Then he lifted the hutch lid again and picked up some carrots and potatoes in his right glove. Slowly his hand inched its way towards the opossum. When he got within six inches of Bravo, the little opossum opened its mouth wider and let out a hoarse hissing sound. Startled, Sergio dropped the vegetables and drew his gloved hand out of the hutch.

"There, the food's where he can reach it now," Sergio declared, pretending he had intended to drop the vegetables just as he did. But Bravo didn't come forward and eat his special treats. He just stood there stiff and open-mouthed in the corner.

The next two days the boys tried offering Bravo different types of treats: pears, apples, and mangos, some of Pepper's dry catfood, a leftover baloney sandwich, the folded end of a bean-and-cheese burrito. But it was always the same. Bravo retreated to his corner, and the food lay uneaten on the cage floor. Actually, they couldn't tell if maybe he took a few nibbles late at night when everyone was asleep and he was alone, but these would have been barely a mouthful or two.

Rudy even came out the second night about

seven o'clock, stood alongside the hutch, and sang to him. He sang "Old MacDonald Had a Farm," but got stuck when he had to think of what sound the opossum would make. Then he remembered: "A hiss, hiss here and a hiss, hiss there, here a hiss, there a hiss, everywhere a hiss, hiss." Next he sang the chorus to "Cielito Lindo," in case the opossum felt sad and lonely and needed cheering up:

Ay, ay, ay, ay, canta y no llores,
Porque cantando se alegran
Cielito lindo, los corazones.

Finally, he couldn't think of other songs to sing, so he finished with the "Happy Birthday" song: "Happy birthday, dear Braaaaaah-vooooooh, happy birthday to youuuuuuu!"

He had heard his teacher say that "music soothes the savage beast," so he lifted up the roof, expecting to see a pair of calm eyes look up into his own smiling, chocolate-brown eyes. But as soon as he peeked into the hutch, Bravo only scurried to his corner, opened his mouth, and gave a whispery hiss.

That evening their parents asked the boys to come to the kitchen table for a family meeting. The boys didn't ask what it was about. They had a pretty good idea what their parents wanted to talk about.

Mr. Ríos began. "You boys have done a great

job taking care of Bravo. You've kept his water dish full, and you've offered him all kinds of choices of foods to eat. The problem is that no matter how hard you've tried, it just isn't working. He's not eating. He's starving himself to death."

"But why? His mother liked the dog food. Is there special opossum food we can buy for him?" Sergio asked.

"That's not the problem, Sergio," Mrs. Ríos interrupted. "You see, he's a wild animal who's used to being free. Some wild animals just can't live in a cage. It makes them so upset or scared that they can't even eat."

"But won't he get used to it and stop being scared?" asked Rudy hopefully.

"I guess he could," his mother replied, "but he's eating so little that he won't survive long enough to get used to us."

"Remember what we said the night we found him," added Mr. Ríos. "We agreed to do what was best for Bravo. You still want to do that, don't you, boys?"

The boys were silent for a few seconds. "Yeah, we don't want him to die, right, Rudy?" said Sergio.

Rudy shook his head slowly. "But what's going to happen to him?"

Sergio continued, "If you let him loose, the dogs might kill him one night."

"You're right," his mother agreed, "and we've thought about that. This afternoon I called the vet. He said he knows someone who will take the opossum up north to the Rescue Way-Station and let him free in the forest. Up there he'll be away from dogs and people and all the dangers of the big city. They'll leave food out for him until he learns to find his own."

Sergio and Rudy looked at each other. They had already talked about it themselves. They were worried that he wouldn't eat no matter what they gave him. They were disappointed that he didn't want to be friendly no matter what they did for him. But most of all, they were afraid of what would happen to him. Their parents' plan seemed the best solution.

"All right, we want him to be safe and happy. He sure doesn't seem happy hiding in a corner hissing all the time." Sergio spoke for them both.

"It's all set, then. I'll drop him off at the vet tomorrow on my way to work," said Mr. Ríos. "Why don't you go out and say goodbye before it gets any later?"

They lifted the hutch roof and looked in at Bravo one last time. There he sat, backed into his corner, his open mouth showing his pink tongue and row of spiked little teeth.

"Goodbye, Bravo," Rudy began. "You'll like it in the forest. It's full of trees for you to hang on."

"Goodbye, Bravo," Sergio echoed. "We tried real hard. Sorry you have to leave."

With that, they lowered the roof quietly and went in for the night.

"Why didn't Bravo like us?" Rudy asked as they

walked back to the house.

"I don't think he's the kind of animal that *can* like people. Like Mom and Dad said, he's a wild animal that's meant to be free, not like Pepper or the dogs. I guess if someone locked us in a cage all day and night we'd be pretty unhappy, too."

Rudy just sighed and followed his brother into the house.

For the next two days, Sergio and Rudy felt a little upset when they went out into the back yard and saw the empty hutch. On the third day, on their way to school, the bus driver swerved to miss a gray furry object in the street. As they passed by it, Sergio and Rudy could see that it was a small opossum, only a little larger than Bravo. They both knew what had happened last night. For an opossum who lives in the city, its biggest enemy is not the neighborhood dogs, but the cars that rush down the dark night streets. The opossum sees the enemy bearing down on him with headlights like giant yellow eyes. And the opossum does what every opossum has always done to save itself—it freezes and plays dead. But this enemy doesn't sniff him and walk away. It just keeps coming.

Rudy opened his mouth to speak.

"Don't say it, Rudy. I was thinking the same thing. Bravo's lucky to be where he is."

Sergio and Rudy smiled, happy their opossum visitor was sleeping safely somewhere hanging from a forest tree.